Library of Congress Cataloging-in-Publication Data Available

2   4   6   8   10   9   7   5   3   1

Published by Sterling Publishing Co., Inc.
387 Park Avenue South, New York, NY 10016
Illustration copyright © 2004 by Rick Brown
Distributed in Canada by Sterling Publishing
c/o Canadian Manda Group, One Atlantic Avenue, Suite 105
Toronto, Ontario, Canada M6K 3E7
Distributed in Great Britain and Europe by Chris Lloyd at Orca Book
Services, Stanley House, Fleets Lane, Poole BH15 3AJ, England
Distributed in Australia by Capricorn Link (Australia) Pty. Ltd.
P.O. Box 704, Windsor, NSW 2756, Australia

Printed in China

Sterling ISBN 1-4027-1792-X

Who Built the Ark?

Illustrated by Rick Brown

Sterling Publishing Co., Inc.

New York

Who built the ark? Noah, Noah!
Who built the ark?
Brother Noah built the ark.

Now, didn't old Noah build the ark?
Built it out of a hickory bark.

And every time that hammer ring,
Noah shout and-a Noah sing.

He built it long, both wide and tall,
Plenty of room for the large and small.

He found him an axe and hammer too,
Began to cut and began to hew.

Now in come the animals two by two,
Hippopotamus and kangaroo.

Now in come the animals three by three,
Two big cats and a bumblebee.

Now in come the animals ten by ten,
Five black roosters and five black hens.

Now Noah says, go shut the door,
The rain's started dropping. . .

and we can't take more!